THE HAPPY TIMES PLAYERS PRESENT

The Golden Rule

Coloring Book

written by Dana Stewart
illustrated by Jodie McCallum

The Standard Publishing Company, Cincinnati, Ohio
A division of Standex International Corporation
© 1995 by The Standard Publishing Company
Printed in the United States of America
ISBN 0-7847-0278-0

Jesus taught us a way to make every day happy.

It's called . . .

. . . the Golden Rule!

Let's see . . . three cookies but *four* friends.
Remember the Golden Rule!

Share with your friends just the way you want them
to share with you. Mmmm, good cookies!

Ouch! Jeff fell down and scraped his knee.
Remember the Golden Rule!

Help others just the way you want them to help you.
There, that feels better already.

Someone new has come to our class.
Remember the Golden Rule!

Be a friend to others just the way you want them
to be a friend to you. Would you like to play with me?

Uh-oh! Molly knocked down Jason's blocks.
Remember the Golden Rule!

Say "I'm sorry" to others just the way you want them
to say "I'm sorry" to you.
Let's build the tower again. I'll help you.

Today is Katie's birthday.
Remember the Golden Rule!

Show love to others just the way you want them
to show love to you.
Happy birthday, Katie! Here's a present for you!

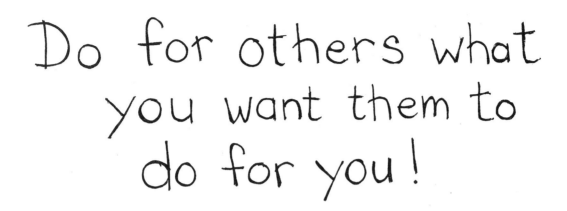

Do for others what you want them to do for you!